The sun did not shine.

It was too wet to play.

So we sat in the house

All that cold, cold, wet day.

I sat there with Sally.

We sat there, we two.

And I said, "How I wish

We had something to do!"

Too wet to go out

And too cold to play ball.

So we sat in the house.

We did nothing at all.

So all we could do was to

Sit!

Sit!

Sit!

Sit!

And we did not like it.

Not one little bit.

And then

Something went BUMP!

How that bump made us jump!

We looked!

Then we saw him step in on the mat!

We looked!

And we saw him!

The Cat in the Hat!

And he said to us,

"Why do you sit there like that?"

"I know it is wet

And the sun is not sunny.

But we can have

Lots of good fun that is funny!"

"I know some good games we could play,"

Said the cat.

"I know some new tricks,"

Said the Cat in the Hat.

"A lot of good tricks.

I will show them to you.

Your mother

Will not mind at all if I do."

Then Sally and I

Did not know what to say.

Our mother was out of the house

For the day.

But our fish said, "No! No!

Make that cat go away!

Tell that Cat in the Hat

You do NOT want to play.

He should not be here.

He should not be about.

He should not be here

When your mother is out!"

It's a cold and wet day when the Cat in the Hat comes to play.
Brighten up this picture by colouring it in!

Can you spot five differences
between these two pictures?

HERE COMES THE
CAT IN THE HAT!

HERE COMES THE
CAT IN THE HAT.

The Cat is doing a balancing act with a cup of tea on his hat.
Colour him in!

Unscramble the names of the cat's playthings

OSKOB   _ _ _ _ _

BURMLEAL   _ _ _ _ _ _ _ _

PUC   _ _ _

LABL   _ _ _ _

ISFH   _ _ _ _

NAF   _ _ _

KECA   _ _ _ _

KARE   _ _ _ _

TOAB   _ _ _ _

RYAT   _ _ _ _

19

The fish is very cross! Use the pile of words to help you complete what the fish is trying to say to the children.

not
play
cat
mother
about
fish
out
Hat

But our _____ said, "No! No!
Make that ___ go away!
Tell that Cat in the ___
You do NOT want to _____.
He should ___ be here.
He shouldn't be _____.
He should not be here
When your _____ is ___!"

Can you copy this picture of him into the grid below?

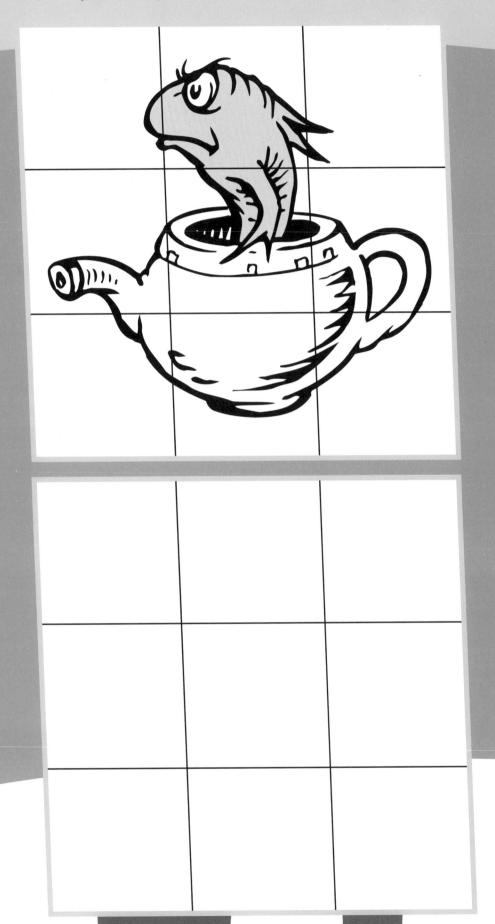

"Now! Now! Have no fear.
Have no fear!" said the cat.
"My tricks are not bad,"
Said the Cat in the Hat.
"Why, we can have
Lots of good fun, if you wish,
With a game that I call
Up-up-up with a fish!"

"Put me down!" said the fish.
"This is no fun at all!
Put me down!" said the fish.
"I do NOT wish to fall!"

"Have no fear!" said the cat.

"I will not let you fall.

I will hold you up high

As I stand on a ball.

With a book on one hand!

And a cup on my hat!

But that is not ALL I can do!"

Said the cat . . .

"Look at me!

Look at me now!" said the cat.

"With a cup and a cake

On the top of my hat!

I can hold up TWO books!

I can hold up the fish!

And a little toy ship!

And some milk on a dish!

And look!

I can hop up and down on the ball!

But that is not all!

Oh, no.

That is not all . . .

"Look at me!

Look at me!

Look at me NOW!

It is fun to have fun

But you have to know how.

I can hold up the cup

And the milk and the cake!

I can hold up these books!

And the fish on a rake!

I can hold the toy ship

And a little toy man!

And look! With my tail

I can hold a red fan!

I can fan with the fan

As I hop on the ball!

But that is not all.

Oh, no.

That is not all. . . ."

That is what the cat said . . .

Then he fell on his head!

He came down with a bump

From up there on the ball.

And Sally and I,

We saw ALL the things fall!

And our fish came down, too.

He fell into a pot!

He said, "Do I like this?

Oh, no! I do not.

This is not a good game,"

Said our fish as he lit.

"No, I do not like it,

Not one little bit!"

"Now look what you did!"
Said the fish to the cat.
"Now look at this house!
Look at this! Look at that!
You sank our toy ship,
Sank it deep in the cake.
You shook up our house
And you bent our new rake
You SHOULD NOT be here
When our mother is not.
You get out of this house!"
Said the fish in the pot.

Oh, dear. It looks like the Cat in the Hat
has picked up too many things to play with!

Colour in the Cat in the Hat and his playthings before he falls.

Can you spot all the items the Cat was juggling
in this wordsearch? Look carefully to find these words.

ball	cup	picture
book	dress	rake
box	fan	ship
cake	fish	toy
clock	kite	umbrella

Look up, down, side to side, diagonally and even backwards!

P	P	P	V	B	J	U	F	J	T
I	I	U	A	H	L	M	L	O	V
P	U	H	C	Z	U	B	Y	J	R
Y	H	U	S	R	L	R	P	P	R
B	A	L	L	N	I	E	W	L	V
U	H	W	J	V	O	L	D	P	E
M	Y	M	L	K	O	L	D	R	T
B	E	T	C	O	Y	A	U	V	R
N	O	O	W	N	D	T	M	L	E
M	L	O	A	I	C	R	G	B	A
C	J	F	K	I	L	N	E	P	Z
B	O	X	P	H	S	I	F	S	S
E	K	A	C	E	K	A	R	X	S
F	D	L	I	P	M	E	T	I	K
L	M	P	B	B	X	Y	T	E	D

What a mess! The fish is very cross. Use the words and pictures opposite to help you complete the fish's angry speech.

"Now look at this house!
Look at this! Look at that!
You sank our ___ /____,
Sank it deep in the ____.
You shook up our house
And you bent our new ____.
You SHOULD NOT be here
When our mother is not.
You get out of this house!"
Said the fish in the ___.

"But I like to be here.

Oh, I like it a lot!"

Said the Cat in the Hat

To the fish in the pot.

"I will NOT go away.

I do NOT wish to go!

And so," said the Cat in the Hat,

"So

   so

      so . . .

I will show you

Another good game that I know!"

And then he ran out.

And, then, fast as a fox,

The Cat in the Hat

Came back in with a box.

A big red wood box.

It was shut with a hook.

"Now look at this trick,"

Said the cat.

"Take a look!"

Then he got up on top

With a tip of his hat.

"I call this game FUN-IN-A-BOX,"

Said the cat.

"In this box are two things

I will show to you now.

You will like these two things,"

Said the cat with a bow.

"I will pick up the hook.

You will see something new.

Two things. And I call them

Thing One and Thing Two.

These Things will not bite you.

They want to have fun."

Then, out of the box

Came Thing Two and Thing One!

And they ran to us fast.

They said, "How do you do?

Would you like to shake hands

With Thing One and Thing Two?"

And Sally and I

Did not know what to do.

So we had to shake hands

With Thing One and Thing Two.

We shook their two hands.

But our fish said, "No! No!

Those Things should not be

In this house! Make them go!

"They should not be here
When your mother is not!
Put them out!   Put them out!"
Said the fish in the pot.

"Have no fear, little fish,"
Said the Cat in the Hat.
"These Things are good Things."
And he gave them a pat.
"They are tame. Oh, so tame!
They have come here to play.
They will give you some fun
On this wet, wet, wet day."

He's even brought two friends along to help,
Thing One and Thing Two. Can you
add some colour to the pair?

The Cat in the Hat has gone to find another good game.
Help him through the maze to fetch the crate.

The Cat in the Hat has brought something
new to play with. Follow the wiggly line
to find out what's inside.

Things One and Two have come to play but they do make a mess.
They have hidden these words every which way in this box.
Can you find all the words in the wordsearch?

UMBRELLA
PICTURE
LAMP
DRAWERS

KITE
TOY
GOWN
PLAY
MESS

THINGS
ONE
TWO
FISH
TEAPOT

Look up, down, side to side, diagonally and back to front!

B	R	R	B	H	S	I	F	C	P
U	Z	U	O	N	E	J	B	P	I
M	U	M	T	P	E	Z	B	M	C
E	M	E	H	L	T	O	Y	A	T
T	B	M	I	T	O	G	F	L	U
I	R	R	N	A	W	L	O	D	R
K	E	O	G	N	J	O	A	W	E
F	L	B	S	Y	A	L	P	E	N
M	L	T	E	A	P	O	T	F	G
P	A	P	D	R	A	W	E	R	S
M	J	M	E	S	S	N	S	P	E

"Now, here is a game that they like,"
Said the cat.
"They like to fly kites,"
Said the Cat in the Hat.

"No! Not in the house!"

Said the fish in the pot.

"They should not fly kites

In a house! They should not.

Oh, the things they will bump!

Oh, the things they will hit!

Oh, I do not like it!

Not one little bit!"

Then Sally and I

Saw them run down the hall.

We saw those two Things

Bump their kites on the wall!

Bump! Thump! Thump! Bump!

Down the wall in the hall.

Thing Two and Thing One!

They ran up! They ran down!

On the string of one kite

We saw Mother's new gown!

Her gown with the dots

That are pink, white and red.

Then we saw one kite bump

On the head of her bed!

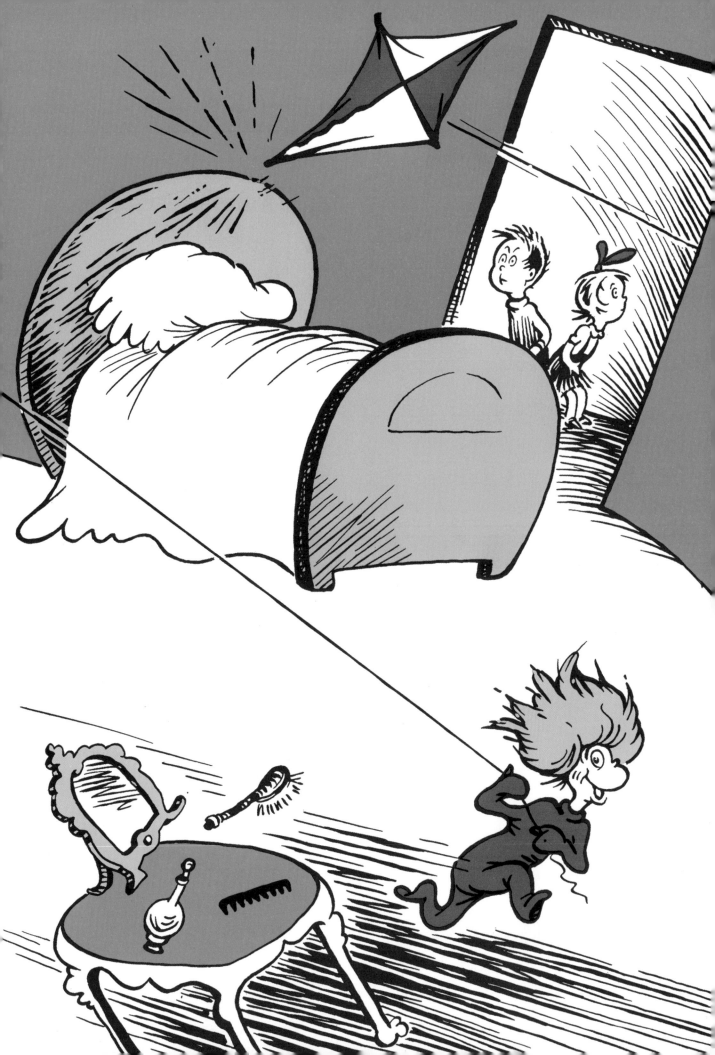

Then those Things ran about

With big bumps, jumps and kicks

And with hops and big thumps

And all kinds of bad tricks.

And I said,

"I do NOT like the way that they play!

If Mother could see this,

Oh, what would she say!"

The Things like to play with their kites.
Oooops! They have caught objects on their kite
strings and they've got tangled together.

Can you see what's got caught and which Thing's kite they are on?

Oh no, Thing One and Thing Two have caught mother's dress on their kite strings! Can you copy this picture of the dress into the grid?

The Things are moving so fast they have left their shadows behind them. Can you match the right Thing with the right shadow?

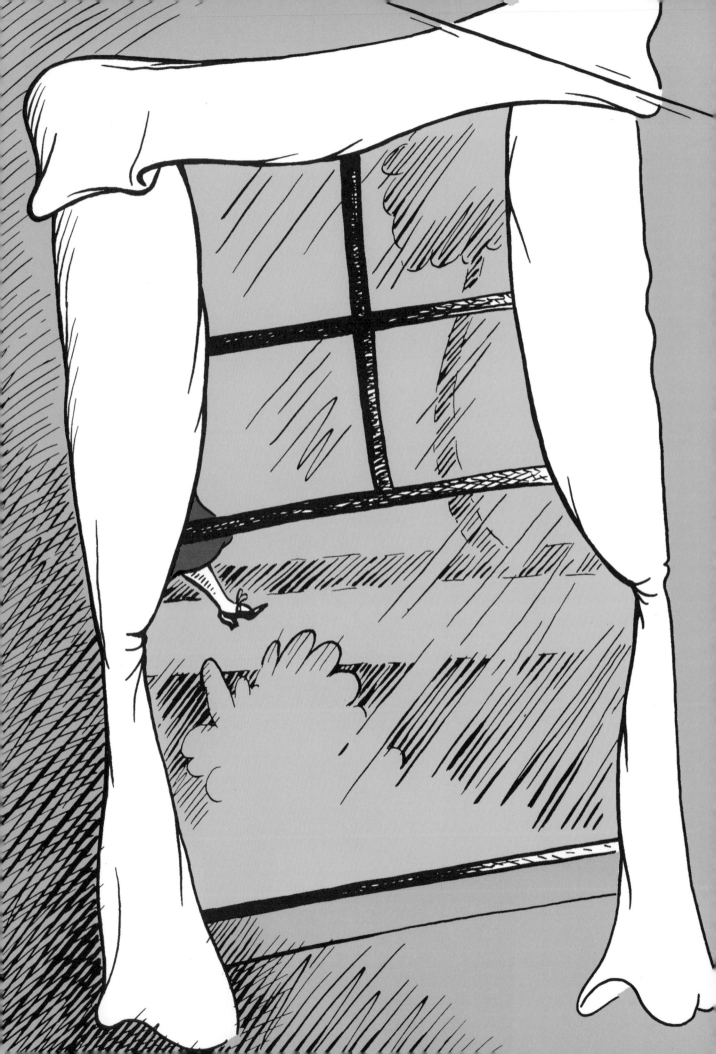

Then our fish said, "Look! Look!"

And our fish shook with fear.

"Your mother is on her way home!

Do you hear?

Oh, what will she do to us?

What will she say?

Oh, she will not like it

To find us this way!"

"So, DO something! Fast!" said the fish.

"Do you hear!

I saw her. Your mother!

Your mother is near!

So, as fast as you can,

Think of something to do!

You will have to get rid of

Thing One and Thing Two!"

So, as fast as I could,

I went after my net.

And I said, "With my net

I can get them I bet.

I bet, with my net,

I can get those Things yet!"

Then I let down my net.

It came down with a PLOP!

And I had them! At last!

Those two Things had to stop.

Then I said to the cat,

"Now you do as I say.

You pack up those Things

And you take them away!"

"Oh dear!" said the cat.

"You did not like our game . . .

Oh dear.

What a shame!

What a shame!

What a shame!"

Then he shut up the Things

In the box with the hook.

And the cat went away

With a sad kind of look.

"That is good," said the fish.

"He has gone away. Yes.

But your mother will come.

She will find this big mess!

And this mess is so big

And so deep and so tall,

We can not pick it up.

There is no way at all!"

Those Things are making quite a mess!
Work out the code to find out how to stop
the Things causing so much trouble!

A	B	C	D	E	F	G	H	I	J	K	L	M
26	25	24	23	22	21	20	19	18	17	16	15	14

N	O	P	Q	R	S	T	U	V	W	X	Y	Z
13	12	11	10	9	8	7	6	5	4	3	2	1

11 6 7

7 19 22 14

25 26 24 16

18 13

7 19 22

24 9 26 7 22 !

83

Help us through the maze so that we can use the net to catch Thing One and Thing Two!

84

The Cat in the Hat has gone but he has left a big mess.
Help Sally and her brother to find each of these items
in the pile so they can tidy up.

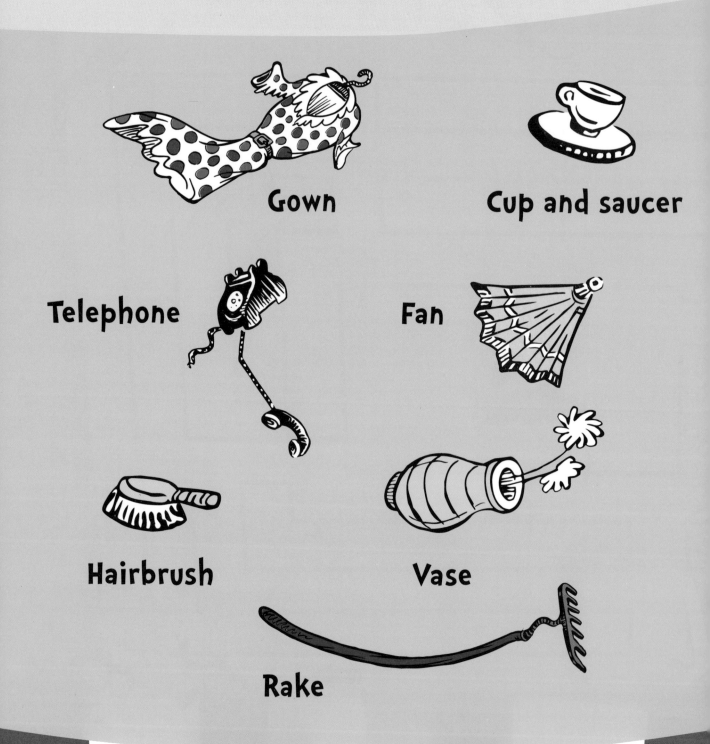

Gown

Cup and saucer

Telephone

Fan

Hairbrush

Vase

Rake

And THEN!

Who was back in the house?

Why, the cat!

"Have no fear of this mess,"

Said the Cat in the Hat.

"I always pick up all my playthings

And so . . .

I will show you another

Good trick that I know!"

Then we saw him pick up

All the things that were down.

He picked up the cake,

And the rake, and the gown,

And the milk, and the strings,

And the books, and the dish,

And the fan, and the cup,

And the ship, and the fish.

And he put them away.

Then he said, "That is that."

And then he was gone

With a tip of his hat.

Then our mother came in
And she said to us two,
"Did you have any fun?
Tell me. What did you do?"

And Sally and I did not know
What to say.
Should we tell her
The things that went on there that day?

Should we tell her about it?

Now, what SHOULD we do?

Well . . .

What would YOU do

If your mother asked YOU?

ANSWERS

Page 16

Page 19

BOOKS
UMBRELLA
CUP
BALL
FISH
FAN
CAKE
RAKE
BOAT
TRAY

Page 20

But our fish said, "No! No!
Make that **cat** go away!
Tell that Cat in the **Hat**
You do **NOT** want to play.
He should **not** be here.
He shouldn't be **about**.
He should not be here
When your **mother** is **out**!"

Page 39

```
R R P V B J U F J T
I I U A H L M L O V
P U H C Z U B Y J R
Y H U S R L R P P R
B A L L N I E W L V
U H W J V O D P E
M Y M L K O L D R T
R E T C O Y A U V R
N O O W N D T M L E
M I O A I C R G B A
G J F K I L N E P Z
B O X P H S I F S S
E K A C E K A R X S
F D L I P M E T I K
L M P B B X Y T E D
```

Page 40

"Now look at this house!
Look at this! Look at that!
You sank our **toy ship**.
Sank it deep in the **cake**.
You shook up our house
And you bent our new **rake**.
You **SHOULD NOT** be here
When our mother is not.
You get out of this house!"
Said the fish in the **pot**.